Kevin
and His Dad

Kevin
and His Dad

by **Irene Smalls**

Illustrated by **Michael Hays**

Little, Brown and Company
Boston   New York   London

Also by Irene Smalls:

A Strawbeater's Thanksgiving

Because You're Lucky

Irene Jennie and the
Christmas Masquerade

Louise's Gift

Jonathan and His Mommy

Irene and the Big, Fine Nickel

———————————————

Text copyright © 1999 by Irene Smalls
Illustrations copyright © 1999 by Michael Hays

First Edition

Library of Congress Cataloging-in-Publication Data

Smalls-Hector, Irene
  Kevin and his dad / by Irene Smalls ; illustrated by Michael Hays. — 1st ed.
        p.   cm.
  Summary: Kevin feels excitement, pride, pleasure, and love as he spends an
entire day working and playing with his father.
  ISBN 0-316-79899-1
  [1. Fathers and sons — Fiction.   2. Stories in rhyme.]   I. Hays, Michael, ill.
II. Title.
PZ8.3.S636Ke   1999
[E] — dc20   96-34830

10 9 8 7 6 5 4 3 2 1

NIL

The illustrations for this book were painted in acrylics on gessoed linen canvas.
The text was set in Stone Serif, and the display type is Utopia.

Printed in Italy

On Saturday, with Mom away,
Dad and I work — then we play.

First we take the vacuum and railroad the rugs —
choo, choo, coming through!
I love cleaning up with you.

Then we clean, clean, clean the windows,
wipe, wipe, wash them right.
My dad shines in the windows' light.

Next we pitch, pitch, pitch the papers,
fold, fold, fold the funnies,
basket, basket, basket the books,
tidy, tidy, tidy the toys.

We hang, hang, hang the hats,
catch, catch, catch the cobwebs.
We even dust, dust, dust the dog!

"I see a spot," Dad says as he touches my face
and rubs my hair all over the place.

Dad tells a joke and I start to giggle,
and I laugh and laugh until I wiggle.

We stop and take a little rest.
Being with my dad is really the best.

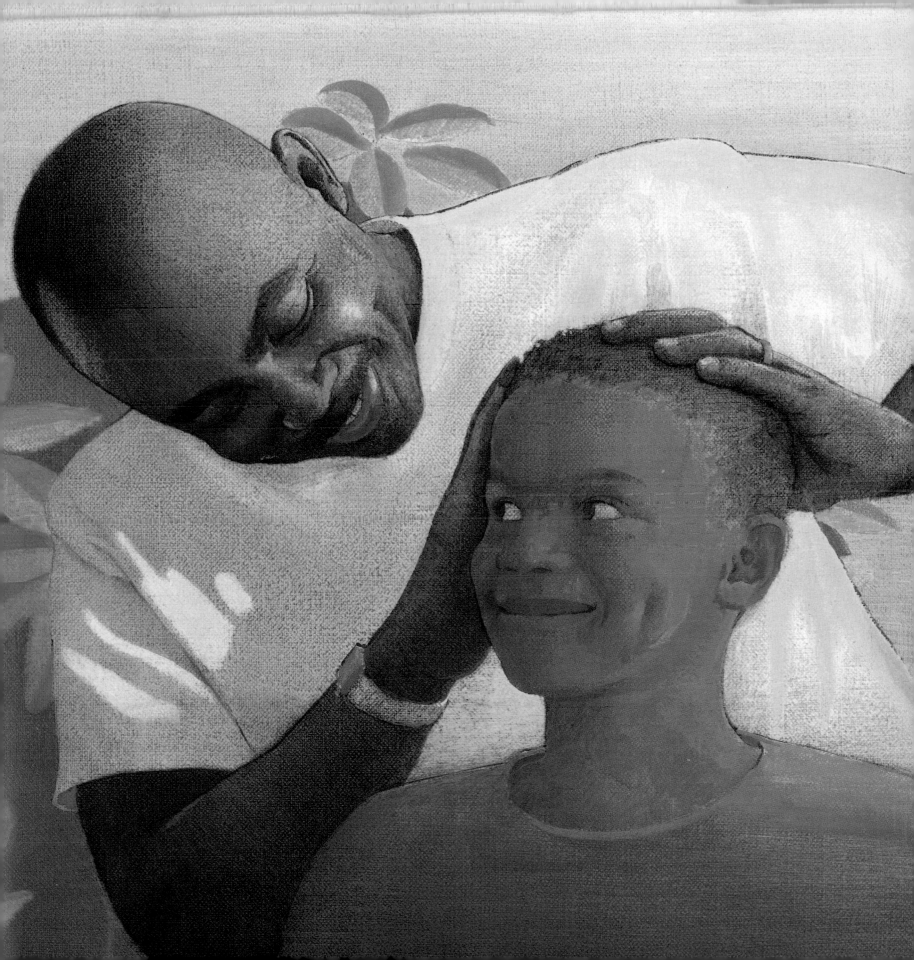

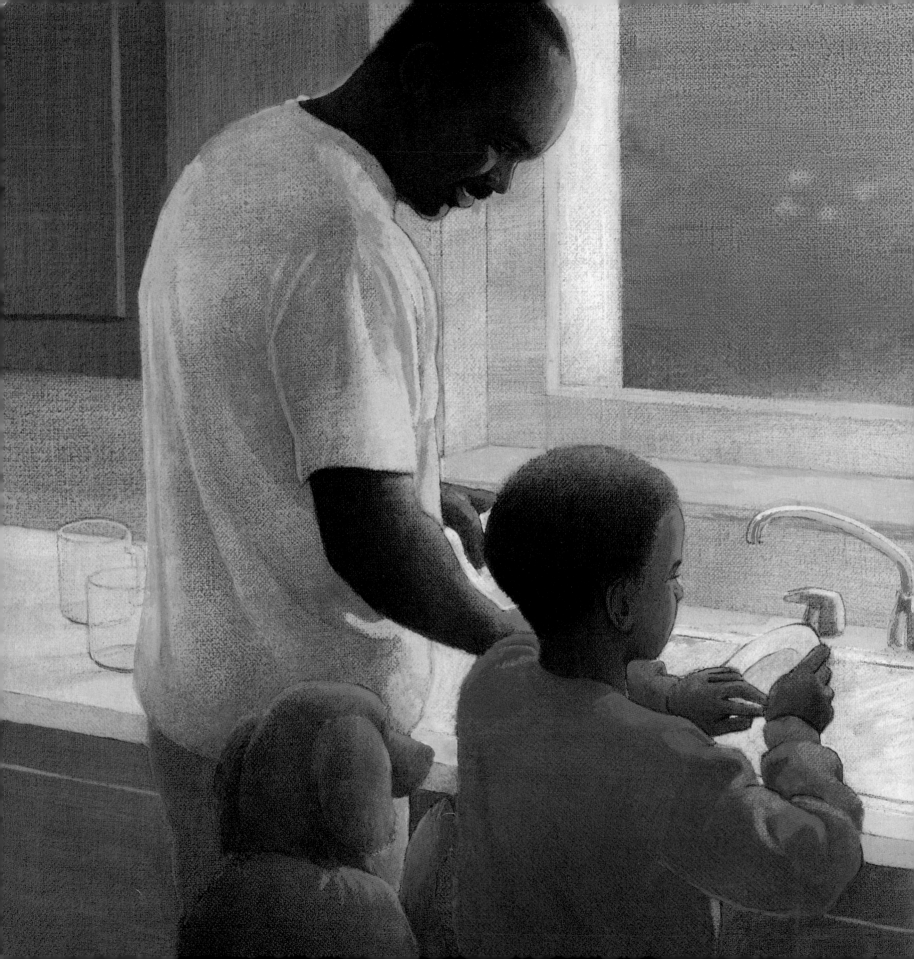

Next we fix, fix, fix the faucets,
squeeze, squeeze, squeeze the soap,
dunk, dunk, dunk the dishes.

We clean, clean, clean the clothes.
Hurry, hurry, hurry — shake a leg.
Last one done is a rotten egg!

After all, all, all is done —
pitching the papers,
folding the funnies,
basketing the books,
tidying the toys,
hanging the hats,
catching the cobwebs,
dusting the dog,
fixing the faucets,
squeezing the soap,
dunking the dishes,
cleaning the clothes . . .

Then to the movies for an action flick —
there are two playing, so Dad lets me pick!

SP

After the movies, we stop for a snack.
Before we know it, it's time to head back.

First we run, run, run a race
and dance, dance, dance all over the place.

Time goes so fast, so very, very fast;
I wish today could last and last and last.

Dad takes my hand and slows down.
I understand, and we walk through town.

It's a long, long walk.
We have a quiet talk and smile.

I love being with my dad;
he's the best friend a guy ever had.